Million
Shades of Life

A True Story

Million
Shades of Life

A True Story

Raman Gupta

MyBooks Publication

(A Brand of MyBooks Technology Services)

First Published in December 2020
by

MyBooks Publication
www.mybookspublication.com
Paperback ISBN: 978-81-948323-0-0

Price: --Rs. 199/-

Contents

Prologue

'Life is a journey', but not many talks about the experiences they earn in this intriguing voyage, we call life. I, Dr. Raman Gupta, a general surgeon by profession with degrees like MBBS, MS, FCCS never knew, would ever be scribbling and sharing my life's savoir-faire at the age of 50. While lockdown gave heavy jolts to most of us, there was a silver lining too. People discovered many positive things. I too could not remain untouched.

My journey began 50 years ago when I was born as the eldest child to humble parents in a small town. I passed a part of my schooling at a Public School in that small town and then got admission in a convent school from 7th till 10th, +1 and +2 at DAV College, Amritsar.

Thereafter MBBS and MS (General Surgery) at Govt. Medical College, Amritsar. Also attained the FCCS certificate later. Joined PCMS immediately after MS and served in the border area of Khemkaran as Surgical Specialist before resigning to start my Hospital.

Life went on smoothly thereafter with hectic and leisure days. Of course, I had my Ups n downs, about which I have spoken in the book further, and which made me the person I am today.

My father was a reputed doctor who opted to serve in the small town in a border area 20 km away from the main city. No doubt I was born in the same town with limited external resources.

My mother was M.A in English but preferred to dedicate her life towards her home as a homemaker and to give her whole time to her family.

My younger brother Rishi a Chemical Engineer (for he was not inclined towards the medical profession). My sister is a DNB, MD Radiologist. My wife Anupma (Professor of Anatomy) has played a pivotal role in my endeavour to write this book.

I have always believed in working towards a goal without worrying about the challenges. My life has been a story of beating those challenges which came in my way. For good or bad, every phase of my life has taught me lessons which no book could teach me.

Life has to go on and accepting the tough times with courage and a sanguine attitude is the only way out. 'As they say, 'Worry never robs yesterday of its sorrow. But it saps today of its Joy'

I had always been inclined to reading and writing, but owing to the professional demands, somehow couldn't indulge or carry on with my passion.

The unprecedented Corona times offered an opportunity to explore this aspect and this is how I could complete this book on my own biography 'Million shades of Life'.

PS: Most of the names in the book are fictitious except family members. I may have missed a few incidents and names to mention in this life story. My humble apologies for it.

Dr Raman Gupta

✉ **rmn_gpt@rediffmail.com**

Acknowledgement

My sincere thanks to my family, especially my wife, Anupma who been a driving force, inspiration and immense help to pen down this ode of my life's narration.

My gratitude to my friends nears & dear ones whose hearty approbation gave me the zeal n push to pursue and complete this book.

Last but not the least I bow to the Lord almighty for instilling enough wisdom, perseverance and thoughts to accomplish this treacherous task and helped me to convert my stumbling blocks into stepping stones.

Chapter 1

The Birth

6th November 1969…

It was a few minutes past midnight when I woke my mother up, I was ready to arrive, the labour pain began before good 20 days from the expected date. Though my father was a doctor, being positioned in the small area of Chakwind (fictitious name), the nearest gynaecologist available was about 22 Km from there.

The night was dark and silent, but our house was bustling with a lot of commotion. My father, Dr. Ramesh Chander orders his driver to get the jeep ready to move to the city for the delivery.

Dr. Ramesh was a young handsome man with impressive features and a built of 5ft 9inches (to be precise). He was an enthusiast and had a flair for life. His happy-go-lucky fervour made all the patients at ease. For him, being a doctor was a passion for making lives better. A medical officer in PCMS (Punjab Civil Medical Services, Punjab, India), the tales of his benevolence spread across the boundaries of that humble small town.

He was born in a middle class of Indian family with 6 brother and 3 sisters, in the humble town of Moga, Punjab. In the times when our country was still fighting many dogmas, his parents made sure that all their children get educated including the girls and earn a respectable place in this world.

Even with the limited resources, Dr. Ramesh managed to bag the prestigious MBBS seat in Govt Medical College, Amritsar. He always believed in working hard and even during his student days, made sure that he leaves no stone unturned while he pursues his education. His attachment with the family was profound, even with a tight schedule of MBBS classes, Ramesh made sure to visit his parents and siblings on weekends and rushed back to the morning class of Anatomy on Mondays. I still remember, my father always used to tell the tales of dreaded Anatomy lectures and all the amusing stories of his professional college sojourn. After completing his MBBS, the young Dr. Ramesh joined DOMS in Eye and later joined the govt service (PCMS) at Chakwind.

So, back to the midnight when my mother was in excruciating pain and dad was struggling to manage the situation, she yelled, "Please hurry up!" Within less than 15 minutes they were racing towards the city hospital. Pains were intensifying with diminishing in between to recur with greater intensity and the tension was mounting.

The City gynae govt hospital was situated in the heart of the city. It had gained a respectable reputation as a gynae and obstetric centre, where Dr. Madam Philips, was waiting for me to arrive in the world. Dr. Philips was a charming graceful persona with a strict demeanour. She was perhaps

born for this profession. Her magnetic influence and clinical acumen spread far and wide.

The pin-drop silence of the city was got disturbed with the screeching halt of the jeep and my dad rushed my mother into the hospital. Please "Hurry up…my wife is in labour." The rubbing, shaky, cracking sound of the patient trolley approaching towards the main gate brought an eerie noise shattering the deadly silence. In no time Mrs. Sudesh was transferred to the Labour Room".

My father was in all-active mode, trying to get the things together and called out to the first person he saw, "Please inform Madam Philips.

In about 8-10 min Madam Philips was seen rushing towards the labour room, maintaining her decorum and strut even at this hour.

After about half an hour, the incessant cry of a newborn honked the silence. A sense of relief and anxiety mounted over my father. A nurse from the labour room came out for the towel and clothes which were handed over.

The first-time dad was bewildered yet kept his calm and asked, "Is my wife fine".

"Yes Sir, she is fine," replied the nurse.

And the next moment my dad realised that now there is an addition to the family and asked about me for the first time, "Is the baby fine too".

"He is fine too!" the nurse smiled.

Born in the wee hours, a shrieky crying baby was handed me over to my father by the nurse saying "Congratulations!

It's a boy! The rounds of congratulations by the staff began and all my father could say was, "Thank You!"

Dr. Ramesh was always a family man but he never knew that being a father would be so much divine. That night, his happiness knew no bounds. His eyes were fixed on the premature, dainty new life in his arms. He kissed the child gently on cheeks and tried to calm him down but in vain. Perhaps the entry into the new world was annoying for me. Though I was born that night, there will be many incidents which will give birth to new Me…

Chapter 2

Beginning of Life!

So, after an eventful night, the tiny me accompanied my parents back to our home. It was Diwali time and the whole city was glittering with lights. Of course, the mood was joyous all-around at the Primary Health Centre (PHC) and a warm welcome awaited us with a never-ending list of guests. Within no time, I became the hero of that moment, the cynosure of all eyes. The whole day the guests took turns to hold the newborn in their arms. The good genes of both my parents worked well and I turned out to be a pretty looking child who was loved by one and all. After a few days, I was named **Raman**.

As I grew up in the lanes and surroundings of the Primary health centre of that area (Chakwind) where my father was the medical officer In-charge, I was mollycoddled by employees.

Being close to the lap of nature, I grew up savouring the cool salubrious fresh air amidst green meadows surroundings. The wild space comes with its risks and we would encounter incidents of having snakes, insects and sometimes animals from the forest, once or twice a month.

I can barely recall but remember the Indo-Pak war days when the ear-deafening noise of Jets used to take the heart out. Many days passed in complete blackouts as nobody was allowed to switch on a single light in the house for it increased the risk of bombs being dropped from the fighter planes above. Being in a town at the Indo-Pak border, we were at the maximum risk. Never knew that I was to witness a war at the start of my life at this young age. As told by my mother in later life, I used to cry aloud at the noise of fighter jet. Somehow the war ended and we were all safe.

Chapter 3

Addition in the Family

Years passed by and soon my territory was invaded by my younger brother who was born after three years of my lone reign. I was overwhelmed but at age 3, was too young to express my feelings. However, my joy on seeing the baby in my mother's arms, with whom I frequently wanted to play, was quite evident. Healthier, less fair and comparatively cool were the traits of my young brother named Rishi.

Just like any unsecured king, I soon began to envy my younger one, as most of my mother's time was spent in taking care of him. The little me felt dejected in between and even used to thrash him out of envy. However, the bond became stronger soon and time passed by merrymaking, fighting, playing and rendezvous with nature. My younger brother was my playmate and bestie. I used to love him more than anything. Despite everything, I was very possessive about him. His presence was an integral part of my life. Unlike today, back then outdoor games were the trend. As per the place, the prevalent past times were Gilli-danda, Pithu – garam, cricket, kho-kho and what not.

A painful incident

Sweltering heat, rain, any inclement weather was never a deterrent. It led to a strong physical and mental physique. One such day while playing and coming from outside I rushed straight away to my mother in the kitchen and hugged her. Something was boiling on the stove, suddenly I struck the vessel on the burner and the boiling hot liquid came tumbling down and spilt. Some of it spilt over the front of the lower part of my right arm. I escaped major injuries to any other part of my body and even my mother was unhurt. But the front part of my Right wrist got burnt badly. I suffered excruciating pain and cried ferociously. I was unable to write or go to school for almost a month. Wound healed with time but it left a permanent scar which later became one of my most prominent identification marks.

Though it was a small town, I got the chance to get my education from the only English medium school in the area. The school was fun but the everyday journey from home to school by Tonga was most awaited by me. The credit of the genes, determination and focus shortly made me stand apart from the crowd. I was a prodigy for my school and was brilliant in Academics, Games, Stage performances. So much so that every event in the school annual function had a role for me in the lead character. God's gifted voice was another boon. I remained 'Student of the year' for many years.

The small town, where I got to earn most of my life's cherished memories was a little bubble full of lucid dreams and happy moments. Locally most of the times we used to

visit Major Singh's house and Kulwant Singh (our neighbour). Major Singh was a retired army officer and Kulwant Singh a rice sheller owner. Major Singh had a palatial bungalow in the interior of the village and his children were of our age. Kulwant Singh was quite younger and newly married but his camaraderie with my father was quite strong.

Another addition to the family

My childhood days were full of fun and I bonded well with my younger brother but we didn't know that in some time the two of us will be making space for another addition! Precisely, three years after my younger brother, my sister was born.

I was told she is given by God as my parents' desires were finally fulfilled. Both of us, the big brothers, instantly fell in love with the little charming girl, who looked just like a princess. Our house was enlivened by her presence. She was the most pampered now and dearest to my father who was overly protective towards his daughter. Her chirpy nature was the source of much activity in our home. She was our most treasured toy to play. Both of us were very protective for our little sister and were nothing short of her bodyguard. We called that little angel, 'Samita'. Soon, the three of us were all over the place, playing and having the time of our lives together.

We used to have short trips with family or family friends to Hill stations or religious places. One such trip to the Barog hill station (Solan) near Shimla with our family friends is quite memorable. The adventure of trolley and trekking, view of majestic mountains, zig-zag roads, cool breeze and

tranquillity mesmerized us. We stayed at the Govt. guest house. Such experiences were quite different from what we considered usual vacations, mostly at our grandparents' house.

Chapter 4

Lost & Found

I remember, during one of our visits to Mata Vaishno Devi, one of the most sacred places in North India. I was 8 years old when we all visited Vaishno Devi nestled amid Jammu & Kashmir. My father had pledged to pay homage, after the birth of my sister. Somehow it was delayed but this time he planned it well. Every devotee of Mata Vaishno believes that you visit her temple only if Mata wishes. So, it was our turn and we were all excited. The temple or the darbar, as it is called, is located on a small mountain top. The devotees' trek to reach the temple, the route is around 14 Km (both ways) and is well-maintained by the government. One can either trek and can also hire a pony or a palanquin to reach there.

We (my parents and siblings) were on our way to the Darbar of Mata Vaishno-Devi along with Hundreds of other devotees (there was a heavy rush that day). Our spirits were high and in no time, we reached Ardhkuwari cave which is located halfway to Vaishno Devi shrine. It is considered to be very auspicious and a must-visit for devotees, however, I was claustrophobic and chose to stay outside while my parents went inside the cave along with my brother and sister. We promised to meet at the exit point of the cave. Sitting outside, I saw some gathering nearby (or maybe it was some mela) and thought to visit it while my parents were inside, I thought I will be back in time.

But while coming back, I forgot the point where I was supposed to meet my parents, lost my way and started crying. Soon, a police guard noticed me and took me to the control room and made announcements as per my demeanour. My parents who were frantically looking for me heard the announcement and rushed towards the police post. I was relieved to see them and even they heaved a great sigh of relief and thanked the Vaishno Devi Mata.

From that point on, it was firmly decided to hold hands till the end of the trip and was a lesson for future trips too. The pain of being parted from the family has well experienced both sides. Rest of the trip went peacefully. This incident became an interesting recital back home to be narrated to everybody who visited or interacted with us.

Chapter 5

The Grey Shades of Life

It is rightly said that Childhood is the golden period of life sans any adulteration. But I had a challenging one. The soon fun life of a young enthusiastic boy came to a slight halt. My vivid life soon saw the greys. At the tender age of 10, one morning during the morning prayers in the school, I fainted and got unconscious. I fell over the student who was standing ahead of me. Some students and teachers ran after me and were in total shock. I was rushed to the nearby dispensary. Luckily, I didn't receive any injury due to fall. My parents were informed, who then took me home. Everybody thought that I fainted due to low sugar level and the incident was forgotten. Subsequently, I started experiencing shortness of breath while walking, climbing stairs and pain in my joints.

My father who was a doctor noticed all this and got me tested which revealed that I was suffering from Rheumatoid Arthritis. It was a shock to my parents and everyone. I was too young to understand its consequences; my father knew its complications and long-term effects. The condition could affect my heart valves in future.

The otherwise happy family got spooked by this incident. My father still held his ground and began finding the solution pragmatically. My father consulted one of the renowned consultant Physician of Amritsar. After multiple tests, I was put on Penicillin oral for 5 years to prevent the damage to heart and valves. Life was crippled to some extent. It was difficult for me to walk briskly, run or climb stairs as I used to get fatigued.

However, my family never let me lose my heart even for a single day. With the unconditional care and support of my family and my compliance, things started to improve. My health started improving and shortly I regained my vigour, vitality and strength. My parents then decided to admit us at a convent school to cope up and compete with the outside world. The nearest renowned school was St. Francis School at Tarn Taran which was about 16 km from our place. I and my brother got admission after an Entrance exam.

The school was far from our place, so both of us had to get up early to cover the time and distance. Coming back home was also a task; by the time we used to reach home, it would already be dusk. Tired with piles of homework both of us didn't get any time to play or do any fun activity. The school was true to its standards of a convent school. Strict discipline for the timing, dress, the language was maintained. Initially, it was tedious for us to cope up but with time things simplified.

The once student of the year I had a lot of competition to continue with that status. The level of the convent was far above the public school in Chakwind. Solving the sums and scoring passing marks was like biting the bullet. The sweat and hard work paid and my rank improved and I started

getting recognition. The ducks in Mathematics soon turned into scoring above 90% overall.

My father resigned from his government job after 10 years of service. He was transferred to a remote border area to which nobody in our house agreed. My mother and her parents were totally against working at such a remote place. Even our education was a consideration.

A dedicated doctor, my father continued serving the common people and opened his private clinic at Chakwind where he had earned his name and fame. Right from day one, he enjoyed a roaring practice.

Every morning my father used to drop us to the bus stand for going to school. One such morning, a stray dog suddenly came under the front wheel of our scooter and I, my father and my brother fell on the road and sustained bruises and cuts over the knee and legs. It took a few days for the wounds to heal as the pain increased on subsequent days due to the contraction of the wound and I had to miss school for a few days.

Missing the school made me realise how hectic my young life had become. Not that I complained but a small break (even if it's due to an accident) was always welcome.

An Unpleasant Incident

There are incidents which one overcome easily and then there are some which leave a lasting impression. One such unpleasant happening fell upon us unexpectedly. Life was rolling on its pace. That fateful day, the morning began as usual, after school we reached our father's clinic, suddenly we saw Balwinder Kaur, wife of Kulwant Singh frantically running towards the clinic. Her face was soaked in blood and she was in extreme shock. The sight was scary for me and my brother and we could not fathom the gravity of the situation.

My father got up from his seat in a jiffy and asked her what has happened All, Mrs. Singh could do was wail out a cry of horror and helplessness. My father somehow consoled her and asked her, to tell what has happened. It was learnt that she and her husband were coming back from the city and they met with an accident in their car. My father rushed with her towards the site.

Later, it was learnt that Kulwant Singh one of my father's close amigo and our neighbour had expired on the spot at the site of the accident. An intense gloom spread over our colony. There were cries, moans and wailing all over. It was a great tragedy. He left behind his wife, two small children and his old parents.

That unfortunate day, they were invited to our place for dinner. Since both my father and Mr. Kulwant were fond of Non-Veg, it was being prepared in large quantity with great zest.

After that incident, my mother got an intrinsic detestation for non-vegetarian food and pledged never to prepare non-veg at home. Since then she stuck to her vow her whole life.

Terrorism

At a naïve age of 13, I saw a disturbed Punjab reeling under terrorism. The normally chilled out state was suddenly engulfed in fear by the most dreaded word, 'Terrorism'. Specific targets by some unscrupulous elements of society was ruthless. A feeling of uncertainty of life, job and business prevailed. The rich and famous were targeted for extorsion and those who refused had to lose their life sometimes. We too were under apprehension about the future occurrence of events as my father being a renowned doctor was on the hit list. Our parents, though never showed but were worried about our education, future and their resources. Somehow time passed by but under trepidation. For many days we slept during the night at the house of our close family aide, Dr Sandhu as targets were also based on caste n religion. The situation was so grim that eventually my father decided to rent a clinic in the city and left the chakwind clinic. But his soul was there in chakwind. He could hardly keep away for a few months before resuming his services back to Chakwind

Chapter 6

Change of School

All three of us I, my brother and my sister were shifted by choice to St Francis School, Amritsar, one of the prestigious schools of the district. My father bought a van to make our travel to school comfortable, along with a few other children in the area. I being the senior-most was assigned the duty to check the proper locking of the door. A change in school again put a slight impact on my academics. The academics and competition level was quite above the previous school.

What was achieved in the previous school seemed to lag behind here. We slid down in the ranking especially me, the eldest and in 9th class bore the brunt.

In the first semester, my performance was below average. More than it mortified my parents at the PTA meeting, the report card was humiliating for me. I promised my parents with my eyes welled up with tears that this shall be the last time they will get embarrassed because of me. Fixing all my attention on studying and following a disciplined routine, I became a recluse and hardly spoke to anyone. However, never stopped enjoying sports activities. I could get hold of the studies with time and started improving. And in a short time was recognised as a bright student in the class.

Enjoying movies on a personal VCR in those times was a luxury. Of course, the millennials wouldn't know the charm and enthusiasm of waiting a whole week for the movie night and struggling to get the videocassette of your favourite movie (which used to come days after its release).

1985 was the year of my 10th board ICSE Exams. I managed to obtain an overall score above 90%. A moment of joy and celebration.

I joined DAV College and opted for Science subjects as per the family tradition. Perhaps science was the only stream that was fed into my mind since childhood and to become a doctor. We shifted to the Amritsar city to cope up with my tuitions at different times of the day. +1 and +2 were all about academics, tuitions and self-studying, which took most of the hours in a day.

I used to ace in all subjects esp. Physics (Bete noire for many) and was aiming to clear the competitive exams for the medical entrance all over India.

Chapter 7

Bonhomie & Jinx

The result for the Medical competitive examination, for which I was preparing diligently, got declared and I cracked most of the exams with flying colours including (PMT or Punjab medical entrance test). On the day of PMT result, I was at my maternal grandparent's house along with my cousins. We had gathered there for our holidays. The moment, the news of my clearing the medical entrance came, a wave of happiness and celebration spread all over. I was congratulated by all. My parents were on cloud nine. I also bagged the second rank in All India Entrance Exam conducted by DMC Ludhiana and also got selected for MBBS in the prestigious CMC Ludhiana, AFMC Pune and JIPMER Pondicherry.

It was a time of celebration for the whole family. However, there was another story which was brewing in the family. My younger brother Rishi at a young age was living in an oblivion world. Nobody was aware of what he was up to. Everybody falls in love but to dare to go against the whole family, is a valorous act. In those times, love was not a thing or status to show off to the world. The Indian society, back then, was not at all open to accepting love affairs and if it were an inter-religion/inter-community relation then the couple had to struggle a lot to get acceptance.

My brother fell in love with a girl from another community, of our colony. Not that anyone was against it, on the contrary, nobody knew of their alliance. I guess both, my brother and the girl were obsessed with Bollywood, they thought their love won't get accepted by their families. So, one day they just decided to elope and gave a shock to everyone. Both side parents acted diligently and they brought them back home. It was decided to marry them once they complete their professional courses and become major to be eligible for marriage.

Rishi, my brother was not interested in medical stream and opted for the non-medical subjects and after 12th my parents got him admitted to a chemical engineering degree course at Bangalore in South.

After that daring episode, Life again got back to normal and we all got busy in selecting the best college for me.

Chapter 8

Professional college

Though I got selected in various Medical Colleges across the country, it was decided that I will join GMC Amritsar in my home town, just 2km from my residence. I was about to enter a new era of life and to obtain the much-desired elite degree of MBBS. Life in a professional college was new to me. The pressure to worry for the career was no longer there. Once you are in you are bound to become a doctor, was a common notion.

A class of 150 intelligentsia cream students with both girls and boys in almost equal ratio. Day ski's had their groups and hostellers their own. Ragging was very prevalent but not as harmful. It was a way to strengthen the senior & junior bond. It had its own merits to learn the respect and succour of seniors. Sometimes we were made to walk on the Lawrence road and ask a girl for coffee that could earn us a snub or slap but still better than the wrath of seniors. Many such funny activities were a part of the ragging era. The harder the ragging by seniors the fastest friends they became later. Life was good, a sense of achievement and learning practical life, which until now was in a comfortable bubble.

Roaming with friends, especially my bezzie Neerav was a daily routine. Anatomy was our bugbear, the gumming up of colossal and prodigious terms. Dissection of the embalmed bodies, bones, museum all looked very hard to digest and boring. Other subjects like Physiology n Biochemistry were comparatively easy and digestible. The first Prof.passed with good marks. We now became seniors for the incoming batch and it was our turn for ragging the new entrants. Taking full advantage of our clout and seniority we ragged juniors to our heart's content perhaps as an act of vengeance or fun.

My father gifted me a brand-new red Yamaha for daily commuting to college. From a cycle to a brand-new motorcycle; I felt nothing short of a superhero. It was my prized possession and no one was allowed to touch it.

We had a cultural event named "SYNDROME" which took around one-month preparations, the most awaited event. The 2nd prof. batch in the medical college had the responsibility to host it and so it was our turn. It included stage shows, dance and singing performances, night parties and games competition. Being a sports enthusiast and fitness freak, I bagged 1st n 2nd prizes in Badminton, Table Tennis and swimming and participated in a few stage events.

Another favourite was, "PULSE" a fest of the All India Institute of Medical Sciences, New Delhi. We didn't want to miss it as it used to be a medical student's delight. Prior registration, in any event, was mandatory to participate and get the entry to the fest. That year also, I along with 80 students of our class boarded the train from Amritsar to Delhi. The distance of 9 hours passed in a jiffy.

AIIMS had a sprawling campus. Students from all over the country were hustling & bustling there. It was indeed

a colourful spectacle. After a few preliminary formalities, we received our passes, ID card, lodging and meal coupons. There was no sign of fatigue on our face from the long journey. In the shortest span, we were up and ready to throng the fest. Various Academic and sports activities were going on at different venues on the campus. We prioritised the choice of our preference.

The vibrant atmosphere, the games and food stalls were a delight to behold and savour. Cultural events, fashion shows, dance performances, skits, song choreographies and the Rock show were the star attractions. It was a 4-5 day's events and the time went too fast. For those few days, life was only fun & frolic. Going back was painful.

The memories were permanently etched in our hearts and minds. Next few months too went in talking and missing the Delhi trip. Overwhelmed by the success of our trip, we decided to conduct a class trip to a nearby Picnic spot, Madhopur, which was fun too.

The sophomore year passed like the wind. Soon it was time for our final exams and we were far lagging in the studies. With a dedicated approach, we managed to clear the exams with a respectable score.

One of my fav cousins Ritu also got selected for the MBBS course at GMC Amritsar. We used to go along very well and had great affection for each other. She enrolled for a hostel but used to stay with us during holidays or weekends. She also enjoyed her sojourn in the college with her very cordial girly group of friends. One of my class fellow (Daksh) had a crush on Ritu's friend Reema. I and Ritu mediated to finalise their nuptial bond.

My other favourite cousins Vinita from the maternal side was fixed for a nuptial bond with an Amritsar boy. Her to be husband was a doctor and MD in medicine. We all had great fun n enjoyment during the solemnising of marriage. Vinita was permanently settled in Amritsar thereafter and became another family in the city.

The third 3rd and final year in a medical college is the toughest and most laborious with clinical classes, case presentations. One was bound to be busy throughout. Curbing most of the activities rather than academics for becoming a doctor needs much toiling. This too was achieved satisfactorily. The prefix "Dr" before your name is a satisfaction. It was an honour earned and was our duty to maintain its prestige.

Chapter 9

Attending a Marriage

After the four and half years of MBBS course, Internship is a comparatively free time. We planned our internship at the same college, GMC Amritsar. It was also the time when many of us were getting hitched. Yes, back then nothing could stop the marriage. You had to get married at a particular age. So, this time it was the turn of one of the girls from our core batch or subgroup. Our subgroup comprised eight pax, four boys n four girls Neerav, Anjana, Paramdeep, Vini, Sham Singh, Tanu, Samina and myself. This subgroup was made in the final year to attend the evening clinical classes. Soon our companionship continued beyond the evening classes. We used to watch movies together, go for dining, snack out's etc. Since most of us were day scholars, we planned a pot luck lunch every month turn wise at each other's place and used to look forward to a lot many exquisite homemade dishes.

So, back to the day of going to the wedding. We all were very excited and boarded a deluxe bus in the morning to a five hours journey by road to Chandigarh. All along the way, we were chatting, laughing, talking glibly, and never realised when the journey got over. Rest of the passengers were irked with our continuous noisy deliberation and guffawing. But we didn't care much.

After reaching the city, we decided to roam around as there was a lot of time before the wedding started. All of us went to the famous historic Pinjore garden, an example of the Mughal Gardens architectural style. The Garden was a marvellous design of various flora & fauna. The perfectly laid grass in geometrical symmetry, bright coloured hues of various kinds of flowers and a serene aura.

At the marriage house, we were received with great warmth and affection. Tanu was very happy and emotional to see all of us. We all had fun memories which we had spent together. Marriage was accomplished in a very joyful mode except for the bidaai when every eye got moist.

Back home…, the fear of preparing for PG competitive examination started hounding us again. And life went back to slogging for hours.

Threat

It had been years since Punjab was reeling under terrorism. Many ghastly incidents had already occurred. My father used the bus as his mode of transport from home to the clinic. One such day while my father was to return from his clinic in the evening, the Bus which he used to board was stopped midway and searched, probably for him to abduct. By luck or as his mind struck he used the taxi back home that day. We got this information somehow and were immensely terrified. Thereafter my parents decided to shift to Delhi and start life afresh. They bought a small house in an average area of Delhi and my father started practising there.

In a bid to protect the life of his family members my father got separated from his children. I stayed back in Amritsar, preparing for my PG examination, my brother was in Bangalore while my sister stayed with my parents. Life in another city was not easy for my parents, to earn and manage the whole family. But a doctor with his stethoscope can earn bread n butter anywhere. My father worked hard and managed to build his clientele in Delhi with a comfortable n respectable living. But it was of no comparison to the king-size life in Amritsar.

Life was upended. The lonely house used to haunt me sometimes for I was all alone with an old maid. Her presence was even more horrifying as she used to suffer from delusions regarding her son who was killed by terrorists. Often, she used to visualise some imaginary persons entering the house to kill his son. It was a tough time and even more tough was to crack the competitive exams for PG entrance, competing the intelligentsia lot.

Life was showing its grey hues in full bloom. But as rightly said, "Anything can be achieved with faith and dedication" I was determined that someday the dark clouds will shed.

Chapter 10

Post-Graduation

Despite the dramatic times and being on my own, I prepared for the examination. I scored good rank in the All India Entrance Exam for Post-Graduation and secured a seat in M.S (General Surgery, though not my first choice) in my home town GMC Amritsar. The selection was a positive light amidst the gloom. My parents were very happy. And, at that moment we forgot our hardships and thanked God for everything. By the time I joined my PG course, the situation had improved in Punjab and my parents decided to shift back to Amritsar. Many other families had also shifted back to the state.

The first year of my Post Graduation

The Post Grad year was nothing like my college life. Maintaining records, File notes, day & night duties and all sort of work was the normal routine. One could feel the pressure of being in a professional course and the one that dealt with life. Soon, it was time for me to conduct my independent surgery. I performed an emergency Appendicectomy as my first independent surgery in the Emergency OT in my night duty. Though I had already conducted minor procedures as venesection, chest tube insertion etc, performing this emergency surgery was a feeling of great achievement. Felt like a saviour for the first time.

An independent surgery in the main OT esp "Cholecystectomy "was customary to be celebrated with the whole unit in the club along with the Boss and other staff members. My boss was a deft surgeon with a high clinical sense and a thorough gentleman.

At the celebration of my performing 1st surgery in the main OT, my boss said, "Gupta, if you want to become a successful surgeon, you need to savour hard drinks or join some other ladies branch." That was the first day I savoured whisky and two ounces gave me a kick and dizziness.

And soon began the parties whenever any 1st or 2nd year PG used to operate independently. A different or new case meant boozy evenings with savoury snacks.

Almost all days were extremely busy with shuffling between OPD, OT, Emergency, evening rounds, presentations and lectures. Life was stuck in the surgery unit. Sometimes there was no time to sleep or even take a nap. By the time I got promoted to the second year, I got accustomed to the hectic schedule but never thought something was brewing in my parents' mind. Yes, they came to me with a marriage proposal.

Chapter 11

Lucknow and the Nuptial bond

My father's brother (my uncle) was residing in Lucknow and came up with a proposal for a suitable match. The girl was a doctor and belonged to a well-educated and respectable family. This was not the first time that we were meeting a girl for a marriage prospect, but nothing got finalised. This time, however, hopefully, things were going to settle for good.

The girl was from Lucknow, of course, the city has its charm and the people have a distinct aura. The Lucknawi style is always praised and looked up to in India. I was excited and nervous too for it was another state with a different culture. It was decided that for the first meeting we would be going to Lucknow. So, I along with my parents planned visit to Lucknow.

The girl's name was Anupma and her father was a chief Engineer in UPSEB. Her mother(M.A in Psychology) was a housewife. She had two brothers, Elder was Computer Engineer in the USA(Ajay) and the younger one (Anurag) was doing an MBA.

We met at their residence in Lucknow. Her first look captivated me. That charming innocent face and the mesmerizing eyes took my heart away. The guy who's focus was in the medical field suddenly hearing music beats of all kinds. Heard of but experienced for the first time, 'Love at first sight'. I knew I had found my life partner and finalized in my heart and mind to tie the knot with her.

Anupma was a fair, beautiful girl of a subtle and modest nature. Tall with a slim demeanour added grace to her persona. She too was a doctor with an MBBS degree. Both sides agreed instantly and I insisted on Roka at our first meeting! Well, I was too excited about this chapter to begin in my life.

An Incident to mention...

As we were heading for our meeting to their residence, while our car was passing through a street (decorated from a wedding ceremony last night) the frills fell over and it was decorated like a groom's car. As if God had already given his consent for this bond. The ring ceremony was fixed two months later in Lucknow. Soon my bachelorhood was going to end.

Two months passed with often landline calls to each other as there were no mobiles at that time. Gradually, we came to know and learned about each other, yes it was a small but intriguing courtship period. She was a soft-spoken, kind-hearted girl believing in a simple happy life. On the other hand, I believed in a luxurious, Kingsize life. One thing was sure, our union would be a great one.

I was still pursuing my post-graduation in the 2nd year. The engagement day arrived. We were to board the Howrah

Mail for Lucknow with few of our relatives. De-boarding at Lucknow railway station witnessed welcoming with the utmost hospitality and warmth. I felt like a prince. After a grand welcome, we shifted to a hotel. Lucknow was a historic city with many sight-seeing spots.

The venue (Clarks Avadh) looked majestic and the engagement hall was elegantly decorated. I was dying to see my would-be wife after two months. And, My God, she was looking damn beautiful and gorgeous in her sari, like a princess. The moment she entered and I set my eyes on her, everything else just stopped, it was just her and I.

Engagement ceremony ended with a reasonably good gathering, fervour and zest. My brother and sister who were previously annoyed with me of finalising 'Roka' without their consent, now fully endorsed my decision. Everybody was happy and congratulated me for finding such an awesome life partner. My siblings/ cousins beheld her for the first time and told me that she looked even more beautiful than in pics.

After the ceremony, it was time to head back and I was in no mood to leave Anupma. The city weather, however, sided with me and we got to stay one more day. Being the month of December, the inclement weather and the dense fog led to delaying of trains much behind their scheduled arrival. So much so that our return train was cancelled for the day. We spent another day in the city of Avadh flaunting and enjoying the hospitality of to be In-Laws. As per traditions we (Me and Anupma) were not allowed to go out alone but managed to have dinner together with my cousins and siblings. Lucknow's rich culture, delectable food and humility mesmerized us.

Back home we were enriched with the sweetest memories ever. I had a very different and amusing feeling, couldn't believe that I was engaged. Everything felt like a dream and Lucknow proved to be the perfect backdrop to that lucid dream.

Chapter 12

Marriage Ceremony

Marriage was fixed for **9**th **Feb**. at Amritsar. Managing, ordering, arranging, finalizing the list went along with the residency in surgery. Everybody was agog, for it was the first marriage in our house, I being the eldest, our whole family was very excited. Soon, preparations were complete, best considered venue was booked and cards posted and distributed.

And the time for us being the host came too. My in-laws along with guests and Anupma arrived four days prior, I received them at the railway station. The wedding functions were to start from 7th Feb. with Jagrata, Ladies Sangeet and cocktail party before the main ceremony.

It was a matter of only few days before Anupma will be mine forever; I couldn't wait.

The girl's side stayed at a pre-booked hotel and relished the Amritsari cuisine. I still remember how my brother brought Anupma to the **Jagrata**, early morning without mentioning it to anybody. It was a very pleasant surprise. We together sought the blessings of mother goddess. After the auspicious blessings, the time to let lose began soon.

Ladies Sangeet was real Fun. My brother, sister, friends, relatives, cousins all enchanted the atmosphere with music, dance, laughter and hullabaloo. Even Anupma's cousins and brothers were invited. They too witnessed the Punjabi flavour and enjoyed.

Our Marriage was ceremonised with flamboyance and razzmatazz. Everybody dancing, celebrating to their hearts' content. It was one of the most celebrated marriage of our times. In our bridal car, I felt like giving assurance to my wife to not cry and I shall keep no stone unturned to keep her happy. I think both of us were too shy and avoiding each other. Some how, I held her hand to assure her that now she is my responsibility and at that moment she became mine forever.

After the marriage was over, we were to head to Nepal for our post marriage trip.

Nepal had the perfect recipe for this period. Natural hill beauty, awesome weather, Swanky hotels with casinos and a perfect hospitality. A perfect time to know your life partner and develop an eternal bond.

Soon it was time for us to head back to our home. New life, married life was a different experience. It was exciting and restrictive at the same time. But having a partner for life and sharing the ups and downs is an experience worth living for.

Happy Phase of Life

After one year of marriage I was supposed to obtain my post-graduation degree through a grilling exam, both theory and practical. **Anuj** whom I met during my post-graduation became one of my close amigos. He was pursuing his PG in medicine. His parents were in Ranchi. We used to get

along very well. Infact, our **Trio (Me, Anuj and Rajiv)** was known for our strong friendship. Anuj was a hosteler while I and Rajiv were Day scholars. Before our final exams we studied together at my place for about two months. We cleared our PG exam with flying colours. It was an honour and a moment of pride to become a Surgeon. Thereafter, I assisted some renowned surgeons in the city as a part of my training programme.

My sister Samita got admission in BDS at SGRD Dental College Amritsar through the competitive exam. As luck would have it later she got the admission in MBBS at GMC Faridkot owing to the vacancy of seats. Life was again on the smooth highway.

Anupma joined House job in Gynae at SGRD (Sri Guru Ram Das institute of medical sciences), Amritsar. Most of the times I used to drop and pick her up unless I got stuck or busy. There was a profound difference in the way of life between UP n Punjab. It was difficult for her to cope up with the Punjabi culture n traditions. Our story seemed like the "Two states movie". But hats off to her for adjusting very well in this different scenario.

After a while, there was again a **wedding ceremony** in the family. As mutually agreed, my brother was married to the same girl (Priya) from our neighbourhood after both completed their graduation. Their marriage was solemnized with great pomp & show. My parents had a sense of fulfilment and relief.

Life was all hunky dory.

Chapter 13

Bundle of joy

It was time for me to don another role, from a son to a husband now I was becoming a father. Getting the news of my wife's conception was the happiest news. A different and ecstatic feeling of becoming a parent. No words can describe this joy. I thanked her for this priceless gift.

It was 8th May, two years after our marriage, when I first saw the most beautiful person on earth. From two we became three. We were blessed with a baby girl after a normal delivery. I could not believe I had become a father. Suddenly a feeling of pride and maturity traversed through my body. Holding my daughter in my arms was an indescribable feeling, a moment of bliss. Now I know, how my father must have felt that night when he held me for the first time.

Our daughter had most of her features like Anupma, very Fair and beautiful. We named her Arushi (meaning the first ray of sun), our bundle of joy. Her presence enlivened our home with her innocent chirpiness. Her arrival was a full-time job. She was very active, naughty and bubbly. All the time she wanted to do something or other. Life just changed after her arrival, happiness had a new definition... for us it was just Arushi.

She was very lucky for me as I got selected in PCMS(Punjab Civil Medical Services) and joined Govt service in the same year.

Arushi's first birthday was celebrated with great gusto n fervour. We invited all our near and dear ones. The highlight of the event was Arushi's dance on her 1st birthday. It was unique because for a one year child to dance was a rare phenomenon. The epic moment was captured in pictures and video camera.

Life went on, Anupma wanted to do Post-Graduation. She started preparing for the entrance exam. By this time she was expecting our second baby. It was a very tough job for her to study and manage household chores during her pregnancy.

She managed everything well and appeared for her entrance exam during the ninth month of pregnancy.

Another addition to the family

Two years after Arushi's birth, we were blessed with a Baby Boy. Our joy knew no bounds. I had become a father for the second time. We named him Raghav. Unlike Arushi, Raghav was a calm child and hardly created any fuss. His demands were very less. It was very easy to handle him as compared to Arushi. Or, because it was our second time, we were trained to handle a child. We used to call him an angel child. Arushi was even more excited and surprised to find a new small baby besides her. Her reactions were strange and mixed.

After our son's birth, Anupma joined M.S (Anatomy) at my alma mater, GMC Amritsar. She pursued her Post Graduation along with taking care of the home and two children. But hats off to her diligence and perseverance.

Chapter 14

Happy and Prosperous shades of life

Soon the life was sailing on its own pace and we got attuned to our routine. For me, it was managing profession, family, and social life. After some time, I got transferred to 60 km from our residence, it was a government job so the transfer was unavoidable. Commuting every day up and down along with the rush of patients and surgeries was taking a toll on my mind and body.

I decided to quit the job and start my hospital. After a few years of speculation, I decided to go back to the same small town (Chakwind) where my father practised and I was born for we enjoyed a good clientele in that area. Few years down the lane saw a double-storeyed hospital erected on the main road towards Amritsar... 'Gupta Hospital'

Anupma had also completed her Post-Graduation and joined me in the hospital. By the Grace of God and well wishes of near and dear ones, our venture got a healthy start right from the beginning. We got very busy coping up with the increasing rush of patients, surgeries and emergencies. Sometimes it used to be a continuous day and night affair.

Life was blessed with all types of amenities and facilities except that my hospital was 20 km from the city and commuting from my house to the hospital was getting unmanageable. So, we decided to shift in the hospital premises and utilised the first floor as our residence. My brother, sister and parents stayed at Amritsar.

A recreation trip to the city was mandatory almost every day. One of our close couple friends, Rajiv and Sarita visited us often. We all used to have great fun and good times. Rajiv was an orthopaedic surgeon. He also used to examine patients and operate at my hospital.

Meanwhile, my brother shifted to Delhi to run his own business in the Real Estate. Delhi witnessed a boom in this business at that time, and he grabbed the opportunity at the right time. It was our cousins from the paternal side who were already in this business and had flourished very well. They had shifted from Punjab to Delhi during the riots. Rishi got lured by their flamboyant flair and extravagant lifestyle and had shunned the idea of a job in his branch of chemical engineering. He attained success in a short time. We were very happy for him, especially my father.

At Chakwind, managing hospital, children, day and night influx of patients was keeping both of us on our feet round the clock. In fact, it was tougher for Anupma in this different milieu. Few jokes used to surface up in between owing to the marked difference in the Hindi- Punjabi accent and language. But shortly she earned a good name n fame in the area by virtue of her soft speaking, caring nature and an adept clinical acumen.

Our children reached the school-going age and we got them admitted in one of the best schools in Amritsar. A private vehicle was hired for the daily commuting, their routine reminded me of my school days. For the extracurricular activities as swimming etc my wife used to take them again to the city in the evening.

Their struggle in adjusting to school routine, their small triumphs became the best memories which are still afresh. Both the kids did well. Side by side excelling in studies, my daughter bagged the first prize in district swimming while my son stood first in district badminton championship.

Another Wedding...

Now that both I and my brother were married and settled in life, my parents began the search for a suitable boy for our younger sister, Samita. She had completed her MBBS, followed by DNB in Radiology and since she had not zeroed down anyone, we had to do that for her. With the grace of God, we found a very suitable match for her. The boy, Rikki, himself was a General surgeon and his father was a very respectable and renowned orthopaedic surgeon and mother was a gynaecologist.

Marriage was held at a huge sprawling resort with a behemoth gathering in Ludhiana. It was a true example of a great Indian wedding. The groom side was a big family with huge social contacts. With her marriage, we all were quite relieved.

Chapter 15

International Trip

After the extravagant wedding, we all wanted to have some quiet time. I planned our first international trip to Singapore, Malaysia with Anupma and our children. Singapore was like a paradise city. Sentosa, Merlion, Singapore Zoo, Botanical Gardens, Orchard Road were a sight to watch and experience. Kuala Lumpur was not of much interest if it is on your list after Singapore. But the Zenting Highlands was super fun with shopping malls, theme parks, Plush hotels, Casinos and much more. Zenting was a thrilling feeling of being in the new world or heaven in the sky. Children were very excited and enjoyed thoroughly on the joyous rides. The trip was a break from the mundane life.

We decided to plan foreign trips often to satisfy our urge to see the world.

Dubai Trip

Six months later I planned another trip with my family, parents, my sister and her husband Rikki to Dubai, Sharjah

The flight was from Amritsar direct to Sharjah. Those days it was mandatory to confirm the ticket 2-3 days before the departure. Our travel agent contacted viral fever a few days before our scheduled departure. Being ill, he forgot to confirm our tickets.

With packed bags, excitement and anticipation we reached Amritsar airport three hours before the take-off, as per international travel guidelines. We were flabbergasted to know that we didn't have a seat in the Aircraft. At first, we could not fathom the situation. An argument ensued, we were perplexed. I called our travel agent, he was unaware and felt sorry. From the airport, we reached his office in a perturbed, frenzied state. Heated words were exchanged. He apologized humbly and offered us a flight from Delhi to Dubai which was supposed to leave in the morning.

I was exasperated and not ready to decide anything. My brother in Law and parents persuaded me to accept the offer. I contemplated not to spoil the whole trip and yielded. Soon, we started the overnight journey. As we reached Panipat, I woke up with a sudden jerk and found that the driver had dozed off due to his prolonged driving and hit the divider in between the four-lane road. Thankfully no one was hurt. We wondered what was in our fate for this trip, whether we will make it or not. I took to the driving seat and helmed the wheel for the rest of the distance to the Indira Gandhi International Airport, Delhi.

We heaved a sigh of relief and thanked God after reaching safely to the airport after the unwanted hiatus.

After a rest of 2 hours, we boarded the flight to Dubai and flew off. The flight was a luxury and much superior. The

seats were in business class for our travel agent couldn't get economy at the last hour.

Dubai Airport was a sight to behold and our tiredness vanished immediately. The glittering city, ultramodern architecture, skyscrapers were amazing. The hotel too was classy. The city of Dubai was full of things to do for a traveller. Desert safari was thrilling and a bit scary too for the first-timers like us. Whenever the Landcruiser jumped and dived over the dunes our hearts skipped many beats. The adventure, however, was a unique experience. Belly dancing show was sensuous and exciting amidst the dunes of deserts. Donning the attire of Sheikhs and clicking pictures was amusing.

A haven for shopping lovers, we shopped to our heart's content. After the day we all had a new mobile phone in our hands and loads of other shopping bags to carry back home. We stayed at Sharjah for two days. One of my cousins Kanika was residing there with her husband(Amit). My parents stayed at my cousin's place, while we stayed in a hotel. Their utmost hospitality carried us away.

Overall an exciting, satisfactory trip.

Life was sailing smoothly, but it was soon to show its grey shades too.

Chapter 16

Near-Death Encounter

I and few of my friends were to attend a high-profile marriage at Chandigarh. It was a wedding of a very close relative of one of our friends Surjit. We left one morning in two cars (one mine) while the other was to be driven by Surjit who had recently bought a new Hyundai Accent and was very fond of driving with a thrill. Two other friends were doctors and two non-medicos.

We had a brief break for breakfast on the way. Surjit was driving at different speeds but mostly above 100km/hr. We four settled in Surjit's car after breakfast. The route was smooth and the journey was going peacefully. We were just 50 kms away from our destination when we encountered a steep curve. The car was running at a speed of around 110 Km/hr. Suddenly a vehicle came in front of our car. Surjit took a sharp cut to avoid a collision but owing to the sharp turn he was unable to control and our car overturned. It must have toppled over 3-4 times before finally halting upside down around 250 m away from the turn below the metalled road in fields. A complete blackout.

As I regained consciousness, I could not feel the gravity of the accident at once. The first reflex was to check myself and found all my parts intact with slight bleeding from the forehead. I could judge that I was not hurt much. My coat hanging on my window side of back seat acted as a cushion to save me from injury. With some efforts, I managed to come out of the car which was smashed. Perhaps the sound safety features and airbags protected us. Surjit and one of our friends also came out. But we found our other friend, Bharat lying unconscious. With combined force, we managed to extract him out of the car. Our other car behind arrived by that time. They were all shell shocked. We could feel his heart and respiration, he was still alive. Immediately we put him in the car and rushed towards PGI Chandigarh. And, while on our way to the hospital we had another small accident but nobody was hurt. Before reaching the hospital, we managed to get the doctors and neurosurgical department team ready. Bharat was immediately operated after a CT scan which revealed a large bleed. He had a subdural and intracerebral haemorrhage displacing the brain with a significant shift. His side in the back seat of the car beside me struck a pole that gave a severe impact on his head leading to this grave injury.

We thought all will be well now and he would be fine. His life was saved with all the support and promptness. But God had other plans, he remained on a ventilator for many days. Later he had to live a mentally deranged life, though he could walk and eat by himself with support. All prayers were for him for many days. The incident had an everlasting impact on us. We were deeply saddened. The joy had turned into a melancholy. Life shows its nasty hues here and there; this one was very unfortunate and detestable. We used to pay visits to enquire of the well-being of our friend. It took him months and a few years to recover from the injuries but he never returned to being our old Bharat.

Life goes on and everyone got engrossed in their life drudgeries.

In the meantime, my brother's real estate business in Delhi went to an acute recession. He suffered huge losses and was moving into depression. Since there was very less scope for chemical engineering jobs, my father decided to involve him in my hospital and allotted him the chemist shop. So he left Delhi and came back to Amritsar with his family. He lived with our parents and later built his own house with an In-house school for an added source of income.

Chapter 17

USA & Australia Trip

Every country has its charm. And, the USA has captivated many. It is a huge country with amazing places to visit like San Francisco, Golden Gate Bridge, Hollywood, Los Angeles, Universal Studios, Disney Land, Grand Canyon, Niagara Falls, New York City, and the scintillating Las Vegas. Luckily, we as a whole family got the USA visa for 10 years. Anupma's elder brother Ajay was of great help in getting us Visa by providing the recommendation letter n necessary documents. We were eager to visit the greatest economy in the world. Wasting no time, Me, Anupma, our children, my parents and my brother's daughter (Parul) were off to the USA during children vacations in the summer of 2008.

Anupma's elder brother (Ajay) and Bhabhi (Anjana) were in San Jose (California) for the last many years. He was a computer engineer in Silicon Valley. Ajay took a week off as long we stayed with them and we visited many places as mentioned. Children also had a great time together along with Aditi and Arnav (Anupma's brother's children). The care, concern and hospitality were out of the world.

My old-time buddy n bestie (Neerav) who had settled in the USA after MBBS and marriage specially came to visit us at San Jose with his family. It was a very emotional and nostalgic moment as we met. He had planned a stay at San Francisco city and a visit to Napa Valley in Limousine for us. It was a unique experience. We got a little tipsy while tasting the different exquisite wines.

At New Jersey, we stayed at one of my old college friend's house for three nights. He (Navjeet) and his wife took great care of us. I and Navjeet studied together and were very good friends during the +1 and +2 college days

The trip to America had an everlasting effect on us and we decided to settle our children in the USA. It was a wonderful experience seven seas away from our native place. Soon it was time for us to come back. Coming back again involved us into the humdrum of life.

And after few months of strenuous work (Same year in winters), I and my wife planned a trip, to Australia and to celebrate the New Year's Eve at the Sydney Harbour. With the paperwork done and visa formalities completed, we were all ready to move to Sydney on the 26th of December 2008.

Being on the other side of equator we were welcomed by a hot Christmas as it was summertime there. Only light baggage with beach and summer wear was required. After a long flight, we landed at Sydney airport. One of our close neighbours' (same Balwinder aunty) daughter (Mini) was married in Sydney, she and her husband (Vajinder) came to receive us.

The itinerary was planned including the night of 31st Dec, the New Year's Eve, which was exclusively planned at the Sydney Harbour. Sydney was exquisitely beautiful. The

City Tour, Opera House, Sydney Harbour, Boat cruise were some of the attractions we appreciated much. We had dinner at the traditional Indian "Haveli". Anupma was very excited to see Penguins for the first time at the Sydney Zoo. We also visited the Blue Mountains which was an amazing sight.

On the eve of New Year, we all reached to Sydney Harbour on time and occupied our seats at a booked slot in the evening. The Harbour was a sight to watch. Events, shows, eating, drinking and dancing, the mood was on cloud nine. As the clock struck 12, there was a cheerful bonhomie and camaraderie. Soon the ambience resonated with everyone wishing 'HAPPY NEW YEAR' and hugging each other. The fireworks show at the harbour was unbelievable and spectacular. Coruscating magic of the sparkling crackers lit up the sky. We were extremely thrilled.

After two days of the New Year's Eve, we left for 'Gold Coast', bidding a very warm good-bye and tons of thanks for the unmatchable hospitality of our friends.

Gold Coast was a paradise island also ks 'The Surfers Paradise'. It had the best of exclusive water games at the Water world surging our adrenaline to the hilt. Piloting the seaplane as a part of our Itinerary was riveting. At night, Gold Coast dazzled like the gems in the diamond necklace with the Pacific Ocean adding an air of serenity and tranquillity.

The whole trip was fun and entertainment. It was special for me and Anupma as we got so much time to spend together, away from our busy life. We returned home choked with a million stories to narrate to our near and dear ones.

Being a doctor, one can hardly opt to take a break, such trips acted as an excellent rejuvenator. The chequered shades of life continued as usual.

Our children were moving to higher classes. My daughter had entered the eighth class. We decided to shift back to Amritsar to cope up with the demanding burden of education and other activities for it was too hectic and much time used to be wasted in daily commuting (many times twice)fromChakwind to city.

We rented a house in the heart of the city close to children school, as a stop-gap measure, as my parental house was under renovation. My brother was staying in a separate home and they were also managing a small school in the house as mentioned before.

Our destiny had something else for us. Life is unpredictable. It shows its darker shades from time to time. One such incident shattered my soul and left me shaken and broken.

Chapter 18

That Summer Night

I clearly remember the night of 6th May 2009. It was around 10 pm when my phone rang. The message from the other side gave me a screeching jolt. It was a blackout for me. I cried with a shout. My brother had met with an accident and he had expired on the spot. He was going to our hospital to replenish the stock of medicines. There was a tractor-trolley standing in the middle of the road due to breakdown with no backlights or indicators. He couldn't visualize it as the high beams of another vehicle coming from front blindfolded him unless it was too late and he banged into it at the highway. The crushing injury of the chest by the steering wheel and head injury led to his instant death.

We rushed to the site. Seeing his lifeless body was the most macabre site. Tears were falling in sheets. He left behind his wife and three small children (two daughters and a son). The immeasurable agony and the unfathomable loss broke me from inside. It was just yesterday that I held him in my hands and today at the young age of 36 he was no more in this world.

The tragedy didn't seem to leave me and I resorted to some binge drinking habits. I thought that maybe the alcohol will act as a solace to my wounded heart but it made me more sombre and histrionic.

Looking at the young children, we had to keep courage and balance for their future. It was very tough for me to cross the same maladapted site of my brother's demise as it was on the way to my hospital. I had lost interest in my work, everything seemed listless and shirked from going to the hospital. As if the smile had vanished from my visage. There are some wounds which don't heal, they stay with us like a permanent tattoo. At one point I wanted to wrap my life here and start afresh in the city. Everybody persuaded and pacified me not to leave as businesses are difficult to establish and now I had an additional responsibility on my shoulders. With disinterest and reluctance, I continued my work. Anupma was of great help to pacify and support me and my family. As they say, time is the biggest healer, well it did not heal me of the void it created but yes life's chores and my hospital took over the intense grief. I understood that life has to move on. We shifted to our parents' house. My brother's family stayed at their place as Priya (Brother's wife) had to manage and run the school. For a few days, my parents shifted to reside with my brother's family as was the need of time.

I needed to move out of my milieu to embalm my mind and soul. So, after about a year in October 2010, I and Anupma planned a short trip to Egypt. On arrival at Cairo airport, we were informed that our luggage has been left at AbuDhabi airport during transit. We were baffled, not knowing what to do. Luckily, we had the handbag with all the essential documents and money. Somehow it seemed

more relaxed without the hassle of managing the apparels n luggage. We bought a few necessary items n clothes and enjoyed our vacation. We realised that only a few apparel n commodities are enough for a trip. Anupma being a pure vegetarian, it was tough to find food for her. Sometimes she had to satisfy herself with fried potatoes and brinjal only.

The ancient pyramids, one of the wonders of the world, the beauty of Cairo, Alexandria and happy times at Nile river cruise made us forget the bad times. Our luggage arrived one day before our departure.

We were back home with interesting memories and the desired change.

A year passed as usual. As if we were addicted to foreign trips. We planned a trip to China with one of our close family friends(Sohan and Archita) along with children.

China trip was indeed fabulous. Beholding another wonder of the world (The Great Wall of China) was an experience in itself. The city of Beijing was historic and Shanghai was dazzling, a mark of modern architecture. We enjoyed a thrilling ride in the fastest bullet train in the world. China indeed is a shopping paradise. We grabbed many items of clothing n some electronics. They seemed dam cheap with a huge margin of the bargain. The Chinese language was a great deterrent as most of the public n taxi drivers were agnostic of English. We experienced difficulty in explaining our point.

Overall the trip was enthralling.

Back home we were again engrossed in the daily routine. Days passed like hours. Another trip to mention is Hongkong n Makau with a doctor couple friend (Param n

Bharavi). They say when sorrows or difficulties come they come in Battalions, And, before we could recover, God had some more disaster in Pandora box! There was more to our grey shades with another heart-wrenching tragedy!

God is so unkind

Perhaps the untimely death of one's young son is difficult to bear and digest by old parents. My father who hardly showed his emotions took his younger son's death to heart. After his sudden death, he became a recluse and silent. Pain and sorrow were evident on his demeanour but unlike my mother, he never shared it with anyone. The pain and distress of losing a child so early kept deepening in his heart and mind.

I was worried and thought that travelling will change his mood for the better. My mother planned a recreational trip to Rajasthan in December 2011. They had a good time in Jodhpur, Udaipur and Jaipur. One day before their arrival, in Jaipur, I received a phone call from my mother crying incessantly and repeating something has happened to my father and he is unconscious. But by the time my father reached the hospital, he was declared brought dead. This happened in the home of one of our relatives in Jaipur where my parents had stayed. My father had suffered a massive myocardial infarction with sudden cardiac arrest on 22nd December. He was a diabetic for the last 33 years. But we all knew that it was the shock of my brother's death that took him.

God was playing havoc with me and my family. I was shaken to the core. The incident had brought me to the knees and shattered my spine. But now the task before me was to bring the body of my father to our home from Jaipur. We arranged an ambulance from Jaipur to Amritsar. We joined it in Delhi. The catatonic corpse of my father lay before me in the ambulance. I still can't forget that heart-rending visual. I cried with a shriek (Papa-Papa) but he had slept forever. As we reached our home, there was a resounding cry among our relatives and all the closed ones who were present there.

It was the second death in the family in a short span. The family onus was on my shoulders now. I needed to be strong and gather courage. I was showing a brave face to everyone but inside I was shaken, the demise of my brother and my father had broken me to smithereens.

With no other option, I tried to resume my work, surgeries and got busy in taking care of my family especially my ailing mother. Her health was of greatest concern to me now. How to make her busy was a task for us. We decided for her to take charge of my father's clinic. She managed it for one year and later we left the clinic as it was on rent. With her strong will and family support, my mother managed to accept the stroke of God well. She kept herself engaged in her daily prayers,satsangs at the Ram Sharnam society, a group of ardent followers of Shri Ram. It helped her a lot to move out of the agony and she dedicated herself onto the path & praise of Lord Ram.

I and especially Anupma took great care of my mother in these forlorn times. She used to sit with my Mom for hours and kept her from getting depressed. Our daughter Arushi shifted downstairs to stay with my mom to cover the vacuum up to one year until her burden of studies mounted up.

Chapter 19

Ticking off the Bucket List

Life seemed very unpredictable. Now the urge was to fulfil the dreams and bucket list; for you never know when it's going to be the last moment.

We required a bigger house. Children too needed separate rooms to cope up with their studies. The occupants of the house adjoining us were in search of a new house as their family had expanded after the marriage of their son. The owner was not willing to get rid of the house as he considered it as their mascot for their business had flourished since they moved in here. Somehow, I managed to convince them to sell it to me. This was very beneficial to me in all aspects. My home would become the corner house along with North-East and park facing and also my wife's desire for a bigger house shall be fulfilled.

I also had land in the outskirts of the city and secretly thought of constructing a farmhouse, to give a pleasant surprise to Anupma on our next wedding Anniversary. Simultaneously, I started construction for both, my farmhouse and the extension of our house. But as the architect of both projects was same, one day he accidentally sent the farmhouse map on my wife's mail and my whole secret was revealed. But this happened for good. She changed the outlook of the project to hut shaped, which was much appreciated by the architect and us.

The dreary life went on as per the daily routine with sad remembrances. Its always better to resort to normalcy as early, for there is no other option.

Dream Trip

In the summer of 2012, we planned a trip to one of our most sought-after destination, South Africa. It was a 10-day trip to Capetown, Sun City and Johannesburg. Children were busy in their studies and also, we didn't want to leave our mother alone. Cape Town, a port city, was exquisitely beautiful. There are numerous attractions like Cape of Good Hope, Boulders Beach, Cape Point, Botanical Gardens, Table Mountain which were elusive from the general trend of tourist destinations. I was remarkably impressed by the very efficient public transport system, a convenience and boon to the tourists. Our next destination was 'SUN CITY' through Johannesburg. We were asked to be wary of the snatching of our valuables and money on the way. There was no proper government transport from Johannesburg to Sun City. As long as we were in the taxi, our heart kept on pounding and fear- trepidation loomed largely. However, it was uneventful.

Uneasiness vanished on reaching our Hotel,' The Palace of the Lost City'. The hotel was a total of 10. Luxurious surroundings, unique décor, fabulous architecture, heated magnificent vast outdoor swimming pool, inbuilt Jacuzzis in the bathrooms and what not. You name the luxury and it was there. Just like a dedicated tourist, we went crazy clicking the

pictures. A paradise on Earth. Swanky night clubs, Casinos, ethereal nightlife, magnificent golf course rated among the best in the world, Pilanesberg National Park, Crocodile farm, Valley of Waves etc. (the list is endless) were like a dream come true. I and Anupma had an overwhelming experience. we were lucky to encounter Lions and Tigers during our excursion to the Pilansberg national park.

It was a captivating sight to encounter the raw beauty of nature so close. Our hearts refused to come back, but our minds brought us back to Johannesburg with a heavy heart and later back home. The wonderful experience of the sojourn was definitely to be etched in the minds for aeons to come. Every moment of the trip brought smiles on our faces.

Again, life back home was on the grind mode. Getting up early, morning chores, patients rounds, OPD, surgeries, emergencies etc. There was no fixed time for the meals. Life was hectic to the core.

My daughter (Arushi) passed her 10th board CBSE exams with flying colours and with all A+. It was a celebratory moment after a long spell. We threw a party for our close friends. Thereafter In +1 Arushi opted for the science subjects to continue the family tradition. Her next two years were to be very demanding and deciding for her future. So Arushi expressed her wish for a foreign trip before the grind mode.

We together finalised the Europe trip in 2013 during children's summer vacations.

Chapter 20

Globe Excursion contd.

Europe Trip

We approved the package from Cox & Kings for the convenience of victuals, stay & sight-seeing.

After the exhaustive UK and Schengen visa formalities, we were all set to board our flight from Amritsar with a few families from the city. Our first destination was London, indeed, a royal city. It has a beauty and culture of its own. I was in love with it at the first sight. We visited one of my cousins from the paternal side who was a chemical engineer and settled in London for the last many years. One of my other cousins had reached there with his wife. My mother who had planned a UK trip and came with us from Amritsar in the same flight. But she was to stay in the UK for the next 10 days with her friend settled in London and had not enrolled with us for the Europe trip. We all had a boisterous evening at our Cousin's home, it was a mini family get together abroad.

The hectic trip schedule started the next day. Some of the excursions were by ship, some by Air but mostly by road. Paris had the beauty of its own. The capital of France is known for its Café culture and designer boutiques. The famous Eiffel Tower with its magnificent architecture and resplendent beauty as one of the wonders of the world and the iconic Notre Dame Cathedral were a sight beyond words. An evening in Paris was unforgettable along with a boat cruise in rain.

Venice in Italy is a city of islands, where metallic roads are replaced by water roads and the main mode of transport is by boat. Having a ride on one of these boats in a royal style and singing the evergreen song from the movie Gambler "woh kasti wala kya gaa raha tha…do lafzon ki hai dil ki kahaani" is synonymous with Venice for an Indian tourist. We too hummed a few lines. Of course, catching every moment in the camera or smartphones was mandatory especially when tech-savvy children are accompanying you.

Our next stop was Switzerland, no doubt, it enchanted one of the best showmen of India Yash Chopra. The beauty of the place is spectacular; it is a paradise on Earth. The picturesque mountainous country is home to numerous lakes and high peaks of Alps. Those who have watched 'Dilwale Dulhania Le Jayenge' already have imagined and could correlate the visuals. The soaring magnificent snow-capped peaks, glittering blue lakes, Emerald valleys, Glaciers and picturesque lakeside Hamlets perfectly makes it a fairyland destination.

The other major attractions which just took us into another world were, Jungfrau, Mt Titlis, Lucerne, Interlaken, Lake Geneva, Zurich etc. All had a beauty of their own and an impressionable sight. Austria and Germany were also on the itinerary. A pre-booked package trip to Europe is definitely like packing bags early morning, running to get the best seat on the bus and a lot of time on the road. They make every penny spent worth if we talk in terms of sight-seeing. 'Leaning tower of Pisa' had its own charm. It truly justifies its stature of being one of the seven wonders of the world. It felt like we were travelling through the pages of a fairy-tale with magic monuments. Such trips are indeed hectic but give one a sense of achievement and smug.

We ended up adding a few more friends in our treasure. Soon we were back home and into the rat race of life again.

Arushi had entered her +2 and Raghav made into 10th class. Around the end of the year 2014, we were invited by our close family friends to visit one of our other most sought-after destination "New –Zealand". We couldn't resist to miss it. This time it was only I and Anupma as children could not afford to miss the classes.

Trip to New -Zealand

Our flight was from New Delhi. We were to land in Auckland.

A very warm welcome at the airport by one of our family friends (Major Singh and his wife) who had shifted to Auckland around 10 years before. Auckland is exquisitely beautiful. Sparse population, very cordial and friendly populace, exuberant landscapes, luxurious surroundings and amazing marine ecosystem, all made it an ideal holiday/vacation place to opt for. A visit to Rotorua was didactic, Maori culture, hot springs were interesting and informative to behold. The out of world hospitality and affection by our Major Singh uncle and aunt at Auckland captured our hearts. And saying goodbye we headed to our next destination Queenstown.

Queenstown is a small town on the shores of Wakatipu lake, renowned for adventure sports, Vineyards. Its ethereal beauty intoxicated us. We were awe-struck by the striking beauty of "Milford Sound" and "Mirror Lake". After two nights, we rented a luxury sedan and ventured out to the Iconic journey of 350 km from Queenstown to, Franz Josef glacier considered to be one of the most scenic roads in the world. It was a heavenly experience of driving by self on the smooth metallic road winding through the mountains with the ocean on one side and lake on the other. In between encounters with the splendid gardens made our journey as a dream come true with an indescribable sublime experience.

It was bright sunshine the next morning, the walk to glacier began at around 10 am. The glistening white glacier was casting a resplendent spell in the rays of the sun. We walked towards it as if it pulled us with its magnetic force. Not as tough as was the stigma and anxiety in our minds. It was altogether a different experience. Standing there, in front of a majestic view with Anupma, I was falling short of words and feelings. It was just too overwhelming. The time just stood still. The whole excursion took 4-5 hours back to the car. With the fondest memories lurching in our head, we started back. Our return journey began from St Josef glacier to the Christchurch, which was equally beguiling.

But as it is said, "Nothing good is achieved without paying a price." Driving at a constant smooth speed of 100km/hour and engrossed in the spectacle of the voyage, I couldn't recognize the speed limit sign near a school which read 60km/hour. At my own speed, I crossed the signboard at 100km/hour and could hear the police sirens following me in no time. I stopped my car and despite repeated requests, we were fined 400 New Zealand dollars. The mood was sullied, but we pacified ourselves thinking what is in the store has to happen and allowing this to overshadow our dream trip would be foolish.

Reaching back home safe and healthy was definitely a relief. Nothing beats the comfort of home.

Time to join the giant wagon wheel of life again. The old saying," You work not to earn money but to justify life" perfectly explains the irony of life.

It's not that we trudged only to foreign lands. Side by side we covered a large part of India including South and many hill stations.

Especially Srinagar, Pahalgam and Gulmarg were undoubtedly as enchanting as a paradise. Never had we witnessed such an entrancing beauty. Staying for a night in Shikara in Dal Lake was a dream come true.

In one decade (2005-2015) we had travelled rife across the globe.

Time passed by…

Chapter 21

Times to Rejoice

Our children proved their mettle. My daughter got selected in the SGRD Medical college in Amritsar scoring good marks in NEET(National Eligibility cum Entrance Test) and grabbing the government quota seat. Government seat meant a five times reduction in the yearly fees (in lacs). My son proved his mettle with all A+ in 10th CBSE boards.

It was a time to rejoice. A celebratory wave of happiness in our home. We thanked God for his blessings.

SGRD institute was around 16 km from our home. Initially, I and my friend took turns to pick and drop children to college. Later we pooled a taxi permanently with a known driver and a few girls in her class. My daughter was happy joining and attending a professional college in her city as a day scholar. She enjoyed the comforts of home, though residing in the hostel has its own merits.

Life moved on…

Moment of Pride and celebration

My son also opted for the science subjects following the family tradition in +1. Two years later he further made us proud by topping in the district in the medical entrance exam (NEET). He secured an excellent All India rank and got a seat in many prestigious colleges all over India. Our joy knew no bounds. Our Son had made us very proud. A moment which every parent dream and yearns for. We were feeling at the top of the world.

That the phone never stopped ringing from congratulatory messages. Next day, Raghav's success was in the news in every recognized paper in the city and district. Few TV channels also thronged our home for the interview. Few coaching institutes were boasting as him to be their student though he may have visited them for the test papers only. The ecstasy was unstoppable! Many parents contacted and approached us for the guidance of their children who were in the same stream. I wished my father was alive to see his grand children's achievements. He would have been very proud and joyful to see his grandchildren moving ahead and achieving success in life.

We celebrated with our friends and family. He finally joined at the GMC Amritsar, our college for generations, as my mother's father (my grandfather), my father and myself were all were graduates of this college. Even Anupma did her Post graduation from here. This was the fourth generation of our family becoming a doctor from this college continuing the legacy.

In the meantime, my brother's daughter (Parul) had passed her +2. She could not clear the NEET exam. We planned to send her abroad. Finally, after persistent pursuing,

completion of all formalities, we managed to enrol her in a Physiotherapy course in Brisbane (Australia). I remembered my brother with welled eyes on her departure.

For us, it was long since we had travelled. We dedicated this whole time providing the appropriate atmosphere and taking care of our children. Even we shunned our social meetings to the minimum. Definitely, it yielded fruits. Life was in a glorious mode.

Now was the time for a break and a trip together. This time we approved Leh&Ladakh another trip in our Bucket list with our children.

Leh –Ladakh Trip

Our flight was from Amritsar via Delhi to Leh. The magnificent Himalayas on the way was a sight to behold. It was almost the end of the tourist season so we did not find much crowd. Leh&Ladakh definitely is a place of unique landscapes found nowhere else. The chilled cool breeze from the Himalayas welcomed us. After the night rest in the hotel, sightseeing excursions started the next morning. Adequate measures and medications as directed by the hotel staff were taken due to high altitude.

Shanti –Stupa that was a few km from our hotel was the first place we visited followed by Leh Palace. While moving from Leh to Ladakh, we crossed the Khardung-La pass, the highest motorable road in the world. Children had an awesome time playing on the snow mountain and throwing snowballs. We too were charmed with their happiness. Just like any hilly areas, the road was narrow and dilapidated at some points, still, tourists were thronging it as if it was a small hill. A hotspot for the mountain biking expeditions.

There was an exciting spot named Magnetic Hill, where vehicles seemed to defy gravity and moved uphill.

Nubra –Valley was a true splendour. A sight to behold n savour. Another spot that caught our fancy was the Pangong –Pso lake. We were awestruck by the scintillating blue lake and its crystal-clear waters. It seemed as if it's the end of the world and the beginning of life. Spending a few hours lakeside was one of the most blissful times.

Rafting in the world's highest river in ice-cold water was a chilling experience.

The trip is still etched in our hearts and minds. The landscapes, the serpentine road, valley views, majestic hills of various hues were a scrumptious platter for the eyes ever been visualized. Everything seemed to be a fantasy. Such trips are a solace to the monotonous errands and soothe the mind and body.

Chapter 22

Life Moves On

My wife was doing great in her career. After a successful stint with Adesh Medical College in Bhatinda as a HOD for the Department of Anatomy, she got associated with Chintnipurni Medical College, Pathankot at the same post. However, after a few years of her joining, the CMC Pathankot lost its recognition from the MCI and didn't get the batch of students in that academic year. Anupma then joined Dashmesh Institute of Dental Sciences (Faridkot) in the Department of Anatomy as Professor n HOD.

Life was in its full swing.

I was busy in managing the hospital. It used to take around 30- 40 minutes for me to reach my hospital from my home. Since Driver was with Anupma, I used to drive myself. My travelling time was utilised listening to the FM channels, selected songs in USB, Kindle books, TED talks, etc. I was a fitness enthusiast and tried not to miss the gym early morning unless the previous evening witnessed a late-night party or a call at odd hours from my hospital for an emergency. I was also fond of swimming and had bagged prizes at the college level.

After my daughter's successful completion of 3 years in SGRD, we conducted a short trip to Abu-Dhabi. We all(Esp children) had great fun at (The Ferrari World)with high octane, adrenaline charging rides..esp the world's fastest roller coaster "Formula Rossa"

Overall life was busy yet, happy n prosperous. We used to spare time for the hangouts with friends for dining, movie watching or tea/coffee sojourn. One of our friends' group (KKGM)named on the first letters of Surname of all four couples with the latest addition of (Manit and Sunaina) was our hot favourite and lifeline. Another hangout couple's group named (Rocking Kitty) was very close to our heart. Days passed and life moved on like a roller-coaster ride. Anupma used to rush to Faridkot early morning in a car with driver to reach the college in time for the morning classes and came back late in the evenings, tired and exhausted. My children were also busy in managing their studies. Our home witnessed a mad rush hour in the mornings.

The old wounds were beginning to get healed. Life was good and back on track. With both children in their respective professional colleges, we were quite relieved off a major responsibility.

Sundays were hectic in their own way as the household chores, which were ignored the whole week got our attention on that day. Also, it was the only day for us to relax and rest to wane off the tiredness of the weekdays. Still, I had to go for a round on Sundays which amounted to half a day. Practically, I had no 'day off'. The hard work paid and I received the award of honour "For excellence in the Medical Field" and serving the border area as a surgeon for so many years. This award was bestowed by the district administration on the Republic Day in 2019. In between the newspapers published some rare surgeries and professional achievements accomplished by me. We were very thankful to God for all that he had showered upon us. I was also attached to Rotary International and served as president of Rotary west, Amritsar for one year.

But destiny was waiting to test our strength and we were oblivious of it. As if the "Big guy" up there was in a slugfest with me. Never knew that life was yet to show some more of its shades and a **tsunami** was waiting for me.

Chapter 23

All Hell Broke Loose

It was the fateful morning of December 10th 2019 when I received that call and life was never the same again. Like every other day, my wife left home for her college at around 7 am with one of her colleagues in his car. I was in the washroom when my phone buzzed to life. I couldn't believe what I was hearing from the other side.

NOOOO…I screamed, someone on the phone informed me that my wife Anupma had met with a serious accident on the Faridkot highway while on her way to college. I got a call from one of my close friend (Pulkit) who received the call from Anupama's college principal who in turn was informed by the colleague travelling with her as he didn't have my phone number. Pulkit had been told that she is very serious. I was dumbfounded, cried and shouted and instantly called out for my children and mom. All of us rushed towards the hospital near the accident site(My children in another car) where she was admitted. Incessant tears, fearful thoughts and fog made the way to the hospital, the most difficult ever. It took me almost 45 minutes to reach the hospital. My children reached earlier from another route.

After reaching the hospital I learnt about what had happened. My wife was sitting on the front seat beside her colleague who was driving. It was a day of dense fog in winters but they were driving cautiously. Suddenly a car overtook them but met with a head-on collision with a vehicle coming in front on the wrong side. My wife, in order to save the hapless victim, asked her colleague to stop the car. As she was helping to take out the victim from his car, a speeding bus from behind ran over her and crushed both her legs.

Till she was taken to the nearby hospital she had lost copious amount of blood. The hospital staff had already infused 2 units of blood(One unit donated by my son Raghav) with CVP line by the time I and my mom reached there. My heart lurched and a lump choked my throat. My eyes could not believe that my Life, my love Anupma was lying there, before me, in a pool of blood. She was crying voraciously with pain. It was heart-rending and piercing for me. I assured her that she will be alright but at that moment even I didn't know how will I take care of everything. I wished I had a magic wand and could cure her instantly and relieve all her pain. The bleeding was continuous as both the legs were crushed. The whole scene seemed like a horrific nightmare. Since the injury was so grave, we had to shift to a super speciality hospital for further treatment.

One of our friends, (Rajiv and his wife Sarita) also reached the hospital as they were also called by the Principal. Rajiv being an Orthopaedic surgeon was of immense help in her management. We called an ambulance with ventilator from the Amandeep Hospital, Amritsar, the best Trauma care centre in the region. One of my close associates Mr Bharadwaj readied the team at the Amandeep Hospital

before we reached there. After about one hour we were rushing towards the Amandeep Hospital. I and my friend Rajiv were in the Ambulance along with Anupma, all along the way I was so worried, praying to God and pacifying Anupma that she will be alright.

On reaching the hospital the team of doctors was ready and waiting. She was taken to the emergency room for assessment and shortly for surgery. She was dipping due to acute blood loss and her vitals were falling to deadly low levels. Around 18 units of blood bottles were infused during the surgery with a full dose of Inotropes.

There was a team of Orthopaedic surgeons under the leadership of Dr. Avtar Singh, the owner and chief orthopaedic surgeon of the hospital, a team of plastic & microvascular surgeons under Dr Ravi Mahajan and a team of intensivists and anaesthetists. I was waiting for this nightmare to get over outside the OT when I was called inside the OT for some important decisions. I was made aware of the acute seriousness and that chances of survival were very bleak.

Clearly, I remember the words of Dr Avtar, "Dr Raman your wife is very serious. The only option we have is to amputate both her legs above the knee and still she has very fewer chances of survival." The decision had to be taken, and I wanted Anupma to be with me no matter what. Since both legs were crushed, an attempt to revascularization was useless.

Our both kids requested me to save their Mom by any means. It took us (I and my kids) no time to give the consent for bilateral amputations and requested the doctors to save her at any cost. The surgery lasted for 3 to 4 hours. I was praying all the time. The hospital was choc a block with our friends and relatives. Even the faculty of Anupma's college including the Principal and students reached to the hospital. Friends and classmates of my children and students of Anupma from previous colleges had gathered in large no.s to donate blood if needed. Everybody was praying.

She survived the surgery by the grace of God and prayers and wishes of thousands of people. We could feel what we have earned all these years. Still, she was not out of danger, the next 72 hours were very crucial. She was unconscious and on the ventilator, high-pressure oxygen, and the best of antibiotics to cover the whole flora.

Anupma's parents and her brothers from Delhi(Anurag and his wife Swati) and USA(Ajay) also arrived. My sister Samita and brother in law Rikki, and some of my cousins also reached in no time. They all were deeply saddened but were thankful that she was alive. Her father showed immense courage n strength and pacified us all. Her brothers had also maintained their cool with fingers crossed. Her mother was in shock and silent. There was a great risk of involvement of kidneys, lungs, other organs and complications as DIC due to crushing injury, major surgery and massive blood transfusion. She was battling all odds.

News spread like the fire in the city. One of our colleagues posted the incident on Facebook and the news went viral all across the globe. Calls and messages were pouring in. Everyone was praying and concerned. Some of Anupma's classmates during Medical college (Parjeet, Nidhi, Anshu, Arpana)also arrived. Many more were willing to come but we put them on hold as no one was allowed to meet her.

Tests were conducted daily. Intensivists, (esp. Dr Soni) physicians, surgeons and other specialists used to examine and discuss the treatment protocol. Weaning from the invasive ventilation started on the 6th day. She managed to bear it. Gradually, other supports were also removed and she was on CPAP, then T-piece and finally out from the ventilator. Vitals were being maintained with a minimum of inotropes. X-ray lungs showed very mild pathology. Urine output and kidney function tests were normal. Finally, she was breathing on her own. By God's grace, we were very hopeful of winning the battle of her life.

And when she opened her eyes for the first time I was there and all I could manage to say was, "Anupma, Anupma" while tears rolled down my eyes. "Are you alright," she nodded her head with confusion and anxiety, wondering where was she and what had happened. She didn't remember anything about the accident and the hospital days up to now. My children n her brothers were standing beside. Everybody heaved a sigh of relief on her coming back to this world. Still, there was a long way to go!

Daily dressings over the wounds. The site of wounds used to give a jolt and cry inside. Maintaining strength and positivity were the only resort and of utmost importance. What she had gone through, was incomparable. All this time our friends were a great support, to taking care of meals and visitors, while I was only focusing on Anupma and her treatment. My Mom managed our home and visited the hospital daily. My sister and my brother's wife were of the utmost help.

On the 9th day i.e. on 19th December, she was shifted to the room. We had won the first and foremost battle of

life. Many thanks to the Almighty that my life partner was with me. What more I could have ever asked for.

Both Arushi and Raghav were to appear for their final exams practical. Hats off to the kids who in such a state of mind managed to clear their exams successfully.

The nights since the accident hospital became our home. In fact, I was there day and night and didn't go to my hospital. My body, my mind everything was here with Anupma. Getting up early, bringing essentials from home was the routine now. My children and my mother performed their part well. Anupma's parents were there for our support. The days went just like that, attending visitors, discussing the treatment protocol with doctors, OT visits for Anupma's dressings. Life came down to a fixed timetable. I wanted to be with her 24*7.

Anupma was still unaware of the tremendous price she had to pay for her valorous act. She had already become a real-life hero. People were all praise for her and considered it as an exemplary act of sacrifice. Print media and TV channels were abuzz with the narration of her phenomenal act of bravery. But we restricted them for physical interviews, considering the potential risk of wound infection.

Time was still tough and precarious as there was a risk of nosocomial infection.

Chapter 24

Disclosure and Back Home

Two days after shifting to the hospital room, it was time to disclose the reality to Anupma. The most difficult task. Various plans were chalked out on how to disclose the news of her legs amputation to her, on what time and in whose presence. We had planned it with two main doctors of the hospital who performed the surgery and my children with me to crack the disastrous news. Though she was aware of no sensation in her legs she could not think of to this extreme. She was perplexed and we told her that its due to multiple fractures. The phantom limb (Brain still perceiving that limb is present) feeling didn't make her think that she had lost her legs. Somehow on the disclosure day, the doctors were busy in another emergency and I had to disclose the heart-rending news to her by myself. She got numb for a minute. Not understanding what I said. I narrated the whole incident. She cried vehemently looking at her legs. We assured her that she would be alright and we will procure and get her fitted with the best prosthesis in the world and she shall be able to walk soon.

It didn't take her much time to recover, put on the courage to fight and accept what destiny had for her. "I will recover,

I will bear this diktat of God, we will together cope up with this adversity and live a normal life," were her words. I was amazed and happy to see the positivity and strength in her. Her will power helped heavily in her recovery and we were discharged from the hospital after one and a quarter month, winning this long battle of life and death. Her parents went back a few days after we reached home.

She was honoured with bravery awards by many organisations and NGO's. Our room was decked with the spate of these wall hangings. This indeed boosted her morale which was the foremost thing at this time. I arranged for the dressings at home. She had gone very weak due to the extreme trauma. A hell lot of medicines, concomitant loss of appetite with muscle wasting was evident. Our focus was to provide her with all sorts of nutrients and to replenish the protein deficiency for the next graft surgery and subsequent prosthesis.

Apart from that, we also had to deal with the phases when Anupma got low in her confidence. She called her youngest Mausi to stay with her at our home who used to go along very well with her. But her rock-solid will and full support of family always used to take her out of the agony. She was an inspiration and an example for many.

On the 'Republic Day'2020 she was bestowed "Award of honour" at our residence by the incumbent Deputy Commissioner of Amritsar (Shivdular Singh). The Health Minister of State and MP from Amritsar were among the many other prominent personalities who visited our place.

Amidst all this, the day of our 25th marriage anniversary was also coming close. Indeed a landmark moment in one's married life. Before the accident, we were planning a

grand party. This would have been a huge celebration after our marriage. Guests list, venue booking, menu, were all finalised. Other arrangements were in the pipeline. But God had this, something else, for us.

Soon the day of our anniversary, 9th February came and we had no idea how to celebrate in the condition we were in. But our friends didn't let us lose our hearts so easily, they planned (esp our close friend couple(Pulkit and his wife Anuradha) a musical get together at our place in our room as Anupma was on the bed. Laughter, songs, was followed by cake cutting. Each couple brought a homemade dish making a sumptuous buffet on the whole. It brought back smiles on our faces and was an evening to remember. Our anniversary was celebrated in a jamboree way, thanks to our friends. It was an emotional moment. Every couple recited something. I even sang a song on karaoke but couldn't hide my tears.

As the wounds healed, it was the time for the graft surgery to cover the open wound. We got admitted to the hospital on the next day of our anniversary, i.e. 10th of February. All investigations were conducted and surgery was planned for the next day. The surgery lasted for 3 hours. Again, she was in ICU. She had to bear excruciating pain. Doctors were using all the possible pain killers still the agony persisted. For the next seven days, we were in the hospital.

We were discharged once the wound was considered adequate for home dressings. I used to get the dressing drum sterilized at my hospital for the dressings. Watching her cry in pain used to pierce my heart. I was always praying to God to end her sufferings. He had tested our resilience enough.

Slowly the wounds started healing. Phantom pain was also of concern as it was very distressing.

Dr. Ruchi Mahajan one of the leading pain specialists of the state helped us a lot. Her medicines and counselling were a great balm and remedy to her sufferings. She even used to visit our home as a friend and doctor which helped Anupma immensely. We cannot repay her gesture.

Chapter 25

Corona Pandemic

We were getting accustomed to our new life with Anupma but no one, not even the world, was prepared for what was about to happen. The virus which we were only reading about in the news till December and January of 2019-20 was slowly expanding its claws. Being in the medical field myself, even I was shocked and perplexed with the news of this virus. It was worse than dealing with war as the attacker was not visible.

A distant city of Wuhan in China soon became the hotspot. Many countries including India started imposing lockdown strategy to prevent the community spread. Soon the governments all over the world imposed a full lockdown. Schools, offices, cinemas, everything came to a standstill. Since we had already witnessed an upside-down occurrence in our life recently, Corona scare was minuscule for us.

The whole planet was suffering in one way or the other. Daily notification of deaths was in substantial figures. The colossal toll on the lives and livelihood occurred.

Corona indeed initiated a new way of life. All the family members were forced to stay at home. This indeed led to compulsory time spending with family. It was a blessing in disguise. Now that everyone was at home, children started spending more time with us and it helped Anupma a lot in fighting with her ailment. We used to play cards, Ludo and other indoor games.

Long missed hobbies due to the bereft of the so-called time were honed again, like reading and writing, gardening and culinary skills. Anupma resorted to painting and I tried my thoughts in writing blogs and on Anupma's paintings. Our Jugalbandi was very well appreciated by all. Meeting with friends was virtual. Long ignored movies and series on OTT platforms also helped in diverting the mind.

While the whole of humanity was at risk, nature's bounty added beautiful hues to the environment. AQI index, noise pollution plunged record low. Azure blue skies, clear water bodies, chirping of the agile winged musicians, blooming of flowers, were a solace. And, here at our home, Anupma was also recovering, she used to spend time with plants on the terrace in the morning.

The economy had nosedived. People started getting worried about the sustainability of their work and job. Many small and medium businesses particularly involving tourism, hotel industry, shopping, restaurants etc were on the verge of closure. All modes of public transport were onto a standstill. People requiring hospitalization for other ailments were finding it very difficult to get the admission and many lost their lives due to negligence and delay. Even the burial or cremation of the dead bodies was a cumbersome procedure.

The worst affected were the daily wagers, workers and the migrant labourers. Their plight knew no bounds. Being out of income and job due to non-requirement they were

desperate and panicky to go back to their home town in far off place. With no means of transport available and no adequate arrangements by the government, many started their journey on foot or huddled in trucks, tempos, packed as cattle along with ladies n children, without adequate food and shelter and bearing the scorching heat and vagaries of weather. Some of them could not make up and lost the battle of life on the way. Their horrendous state was an ignominy to our society.

Some benevolent and philanthropists, NGO'S helped to mitigate their sufferings by providing food, shelter, medicines and mode/means of transport. Lockdown kept on extending as per the need. Social distancing, masks, and handwashing were mandatory to keep the virus at bay.

The world was in a new mode of life!

Chapter 26

Prosthetic Training

About 5.5 months had passed since the accident. Anupma's wounds were almost healed and she was free from dressings. A great relief. She started taking web lectures from home as everyone was doing in corona times. The college authorities (Chairman and Principal) of Dashmesh college were supporting her to their best.

We had passed the two stages successfully and the final stage of prosthetic donning, training and rehabilitation was to start. Corona had already delayed us for this. I checked out with a few companies and enquired from different sources for the best prosthesis in the world suitable for her. Even visited a few centres. Finally, we approved for a centre in Delhi. Anupma was performing muscle-strengthening exercises at home to build up the resilience for prosthetic training.

After a zoom meeting, it was decided that training shall be in the Feel Foot Department of Amandeep hospital at Amritsar. As the lockdown restrictions eased, The team arrived, took measurements for the cast and construction of the socket, the crux of training.

Finally, the phase of learning to walk initiated with the grace of God. It was a daunting task to stand on the prosthesis and balancing the body. The body had not been on the standing mode for many months. The first day of trial was satisfactory. Anupma succeeded in standing and bearing her weight on the prosthesis for the stipulated time. A lot of strength of the upper body was required. And seeing her standing on her own, was an emotional sight.

This incident taught us that, come what may, we must deal with every situation with perseverance and fortitude. "Pain is inevitable…suffering is optional", goes well for Anupma. The second day was again balancing, enduring, getting the brain accustomed to it. The right-side stump being short caused pain and difficulty.

A couple of days passed, it was time to take the first step forward. This epic moment (The first step of my wife in her new life) was recorded by my son on the phone camera. Tears of mirth dropped down. We were happy and thankful to God. Anupma was determined to walk as early as possible. Even the training team was surprised at the pace she was progressing. They applauded her and congratulated us all.

A satisfaction that life shall be on the normal track soon was amusing us at the back of our minds. Training used to exhaust her down. She faced some redness and blisters on her stump probably due to pressure. Her determination to move on was enough to overcome the obstacles. Every day an improvement was achieved which added a ray of hope. Training had started with the simple fixed crude prosthetic legs without knee joint.

After two weeks, the joint part was added but the final knee joint was supposed to arrive from Germany. Stamina

and balancing started to build slowly. Another two weeks, the foot pieces arrived from the USA. They were the final feet of Anupma. Light, flexible and aesthetic as compared to the crude ones. But the emotions and nostalgia for God's original feet always drenched our eyes.

In a month, Anupma could stand without support for 1-2 minutes and walk with support. Modifications and adjustments were a part of the procedure. But in another few weeks, it seemed that the progress had come to a standstill. This was pretty disturbing. The trainers assured us that it's taking the presumed time and next progress shall occur with the new robotic joint. We were eagerly waiting for the new wonder joint.

Chapter 27

The Final Prosthesis

Training with the makeshift prosthesis was complete. The final prosthesis (Rheo knee) from Germany had arrived. Ossur India country head from Mumbai along with few people from Delhi brought it to Amritsar. The final socket was crafted by the team. Our hopes were high.

Though the components were of cutting-edge technology, still there was much to be sweated off. Training used to be around 4 hours a day. First, she walked with bars support, then with one hand support, then with the walker.

New Life Goes On

Our story does not end here, there will be more challenges which will come our way and we are ready to face and overcome each, together with love and togetherness.

At present, we (I, Anupma, my children, my mother) are staying at our residence in Amritsar. I am running my hospital in the same town (Chakwind), commuting up and down daily. Anupma is continuing web lectures and painting.

My children are pursuing their studies and doing well. We are leading a happy united life. Our friends and relatives are in regular touch with us.

Anupma is doing her daily training with the prosthesis. We have installed the whole training infrastructure at home and hired a trainer. She can now walk with the stick. Her positive and strong will is her biggest asset. I am sure with her courage, our family, friend full support and by the grace of God, she will be able to walk normally in a short time.

So, friends, this is my true story. God has brought us on this Earth with a purpose for everyone. He tests us as a Guru and grants us the opportunity to inspire, motivate and influence this world to make a mark before the final curtain of life falls. As you can gather from this story, he has tested us to the core.

A beautiful adage 'Aim is not to live forever but to do something that will! Life unveils its 'Million Shades'. There is no such thing as real utopian life.

Some people have more greys in their platter, it is all in destiny and your karma. These ups & downs, joys & sorrows are a part of our journey in this stormy ocean of life as a sailor. We have to helm our boat to the shore and swim against the tide with patience, faith, perseverance and diligence.

My wife has become that sailor who has defeated all the odds and is keeping her boat stable even in the worst of storms. She has left an indelible mark in the hearts and minds of everyone who have ever known her and has achieved a position which every being aspires for, with her unmatchable valiant act of supreme sacrifice 'The Service above Self'. And remember "Tough times don't last but tough people do"

As I conclude this book, I urge everyone to bring out their inner 'Alchemy' in terms of gratitude, compassion, service and humility and strive to make this world a better place to live for others.

Au Revoir in A'bientot...